"WE ARE GORKS," SAYS A VOICE IN YOUR HEAD. . . .

"You will do as we say."

You know that the aliens are communicating with you. But they have only slits for mouths, and you do not see the slits move.

"Stand up," orders the voice in your head.

If you decide you have no choice and should do as they say, turn to page 53.

If you think you might be able to fool them by pretending that you are unconscious, turn to page 54.

**BUT THINK BEFORE YOU ACT—
THE CHOICE IS YOURS!**

WHICH WAY BOOKS for you to enjoy

Available from ARCHWAY paperbacks

WHICH WAY BOOKS #2

VAMPIRES, SPIES AND ALIEN BEINGS

R.G. Austin

ILLUSTRATED BY ANTHONY KRAMER

AN ARCHWAY PAPERBACK
Published by POCKET BOOKS • NEW YORK

AN ARCHWAY PAPERBACK *Original*

An Archway Paperback published by
POCKET BOOKS, a Simon & Schuster division of
GULF & WESTERN CORPORATION
1230 Avenue of the Americas, New York, N.Y. 10020

ISBN: 0-671-45758-6

First Archway Paperback printing January, 1982

10 9 8 7 6 5 4 3 2

AN ARCHWAY PAPERBACK and colophon are
trademarks of Simon & Schuster.

WHICH WAY is a trademark of Simon & Schuster.

Printed in the U.S.A.

IL 3+

For Noah with love
and thanks for all his help

Attention!

    Which Way Books must be read in a special way. DO NOT READ THE PAGES IN ORDER. If you do, the story will make no sense at all. Instead, follow the directions at the bottom of each page until you come to an ending. Only then should you return to the beginning and start over again, making different choices this time.

    There are many possibilities for exciting adventures. Some of the endings are good; some of the endings are bad. If you meet a terrible fate, you can reverse it in your next story by making new choices.

    Remember: follow the directions carefully, and have fun!

Congratulations! You have won the Grin Toothpaste Sweepstakes. Your prize is an all-expense-paid trip to a Hollywood studio lot.

You are greeted at the gate by a guide who explains that three different movies are being filmed on the lot at three different locations. As you walk toward the place where the space movie is being shot, a deafening roar fills the air. The sky turns black, and then an unearthly glow hovers all around you.

"Oh no! It happened!" cries the guide.

(continued on page 2)

"What happened?" you ask as the eerie noise begins to subside.

"If it's what I think it is, we're in serious trouble. The special effects team has been working for months to create realism on the set of the space movie. They built a special machine that turns fantasy into reality. The explosion means that they have lost control, that the time alternater has been pushed beyond the fail-safe level."

"What will happen to us?" you ask, afraid to hear the answer.

"All I know is that we are doomed to live in new times and new places. The movies aren't movies anymore. They are really happening. We have exploded into a Reality Warp, and you and I are caught in the middle of it."

(continued on page 3)

The guide begins to run, and you follow him. The sky is now flashing with colors. The world turns purple, then green, then orange.

As you run onto the set of the space movie, you feel your body grow light, as if gravity has disappeared and you are no longer bound by Earth's laws.

"Stop!" someone shouts to you. But it is too late. You crash into an invisible barrier and fall. When you look up from the ground, you see three alien beings walking toward you. They motion for you to come with them.

If you choose to go with the aliens, turn to page 4.

If, instead of going with the aliens, you walk across the lot to the set of Nighttime Terror, *turn to page 6.*

If you prefer to visit the set of the spy movie, Triple-O-Three, *turn to page 7.*

As you follow the aliens toward their glowing spaceship, you understand what the tour guide was saying. You are trapped in a Reality Warp. The actors have, indeed, become real aliens.

"Hasten, my friend!" says one of the aliens in a computerlike voice. "We must escape before the Gorks arrive."

"Who are the Gorks?" you ask as you arrive at the spaceship.

"We have no time to explain," another alien shouts. He stands in an orange triangle that is glowing on the ground, and he is suddenly sucked up into the spaceship.

"Stand on the orange triangle if you wish to come with us," calls a voice from inside the ship.

If you choose to stand on the orange triangle, turn to page 10.

If you would rather risk staying behind, turn to page 11.

You think anything would be better than being caught in a space movie that has become real. You do not understand yet that every movie on the lot has become real.

As you approach the set of the suspense film, you see a classroom filled with children just your age. There is a teacher sitting at a desk in the front of the room. The shades are drawn, and no sunlight enters the room.

The teacher, a man named Mr. Draco, looks at you angrily.

"What are you doing away from your desk?" he asks. "Sit down there." He points to an empty seat.

Turn to page 12.

You stand alone for a moment, shaken by what has just happened.

You see the set of the spy film directly in front of you. As you walk toward it, you pass a phone booth. The telephone is ringing. Without thinking, you enter the booth and pick up the receiver.

"Good afternoon, Triple-O-Three," says the voice on the other end. "You will find a cassette tape under the shelf in front of you. Take it and place it in the slot behind the phone."

There is a click, and the voice is cut off.

(continued on page 8)

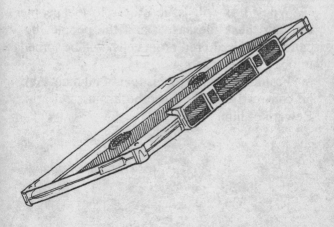

Curious, you play the tape. It says: "There is an evil plan afoot in America. Ima Sneke is a wicked scientist who can be identified by a heart-shaped birthmark on her cheek. Ima and her cohorts, Wiley Fox and Frank N. Stein, have devised a plan to conquer America by brainwashing the entire population. They intend to drop receptor pellets into the water systems of cities and towns, beginning with Los Angeles. These pellets will alter the molecular structure of the brain cells of those who drink the water. The scientists also intend to send out high-speed subliminal messages during local television programs by penetrating the airwaves with scientific techniques that they have developed.

"Wiley Fox will issue orders to the people through these messages; and the people, because of their altered brain cells, will be forced to obey these orders.

"Frank N. Stein's role is that of hit man. And he can really hit, because he has a steel arm. Beware of him.

(continued on page 9)

"Your assignment is to apprehend the criminals and to prevent the pellets from contaminating the water system. If you fail, you must get the antidote into the water immediately, or the city will be doomed.

"You can pick up the latest crime-fighting devices from our arsenal in Bungalow D. If you should need transportation, our specially equipped motorcycle is parked by the telephone booth.

"That is all. In ten seconds this tape will self-destruct."

If you think this is all a trick and you wait to see if the tape actually self-destructs, turn to page 13.

If you go directly to Bungalow D, turn to page 14.

Trembling, you step into the orange triangle. The lights from the spaceship bathe you in a warm, blue glow. Before you have time to change your mind, you find yourself sitting on the floor of the spaceship, surrounded by ten curious aliens.

If you think that you should speak first, turn to page 15.

If you are too frightened to speak, turn to page 16.

You watch as the spaceship glows brighter and brighter and finally takes off.

A voice says: "Good. The Moosers are gone. Now you are ours."

You look around but see no one. Then you realize that the voice came from inside your own head.

"Walk straight ahead and turn at the corner," says the voice in your head.

Even though you are confused, if you choose to obey the voice, turn to page 17.

If you refuse to follow instructions from an unknown source, turn to page 18.

As soon as you are seated, the kid behind you taps you on the shoulder. He whispers: "That's Charlie's seat. He sat there until yesterday. But he was murdered last night."

A chill runs up your spine.

If that news spooks you, and you want to change seats, turn to page 20.

If you are afraid to move because the teacher might get angry at you, turn to page 21.

You suspect that this is a publicity stunt for the benefit of studio visitors. But suddenly, there is a sharp bang, and a bullet shatters the window of the phone booth.

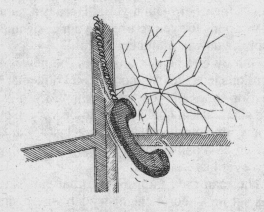

You remember what the guide told you about the Reality Warp and realize that the phone message and the bullet are real.

If you decide to get over to Bungalow D as fast as you can, turn to page 14.

If you duck behind the phone booth and try to determine who is shooting at you, turn to page 22.

As you leave the phone booth, a bullet whizzes past your head. You throw yourself on the ground and crawl on your belly to Bungalow D. When you arrive, you are greeted by a man.

"Welcome, Triple-O-Three," he says as he closes the door behind you. "Here is a variety of weapons for you to use on your assignment. I think you will find them useful."

One by one he demonstrates the newest inventions in secret weapons. You know that the suction shoes and the wrist communicator with the silent alarm could prove to be very useful. But your favorite weapon is a laser gun disguised as a ball-point pen. You wonder if you will ever have to use it.

The man then informs you that Ima Sneke has set up a secret chemistry lab where she is making the receptor pellets.

"The lab is somewhere on the studio lot," he says, "but we don't know where."

If you try to locate Sneke's chemistry lab, turn to page 23.

If you decide to investigate the shooting, turn to page 25.

"What's happening?" you ask. "I don't understand anything."

"We are Moosers from a peaceful planet many galaxies away," says the smallest alien. "We sought to explore your Earth without creating panic. Making this movie was our idea. We passed the thought on to your filming people. Now it is time for us to do our experiments. Will you help us?" he asks. Then he adds, "If you do not want to help, we will take you for a journey in space."

If you are afraid that you might be harmed by their experiments and would prefer traveling in space, turn to page 16.

If you choose to help the aliens, turn to page 26.

"Do not be frightened," says one of the aliens. "We shall not harm you. Remain still while we lift off."

The aliens seem kind. But you are not so certain now that you want to go with them into space.

If you leave the spaceship, explaining to the aliens that you have another appointment, turn to page 11.

If you decide to trust the aliens enough to go with them, turn to page 28.

You walk straight ahead and turn the corner. In spite of your misgivings, you feel compelled to follow the instructions that continue to fill your head. You lose track of time and space.

Suddenly, you find yourself staring at a giant computer. You wonder how you got there.

"Push the button marked X-34," says the voice in your head.

If you push the button, turn to page 30.

If you run up the stairs at the far end of the room in an attempt to escape the voice, turn to page 32.

You are standing alone, trying to decide what to do next, when you feel something growing around you. You flail your arms and kick your feet, but it is too late. You are trapped inside a transparent bubble.

The bubble begins to roll and you tumble head over heels toward a gigantic doughnut-shaped spaceship. You curl up in a ball just as you are about to crash.

(continued on page 19)

But instead of crashing, you pass right through the wall and find yourself sprawled on the floor of the spaceship, the bubble gone.

You are surrounded by a circle of silver-skinned creatures. They are Gorks. And every one of them is pointing a dangerous-looking object in your direction.

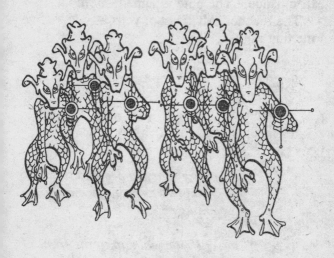

If you are so stunned that you find it impossible to speak, turn to page 33.

If you decide that the wisest course would be to greet the creatures calmly, turn to page 34.

You move to a seat directly across the aisle. As soon as you sit down, a student sitting next to you passes you a note.

It reads: "That was Lisa's seat. She disappeared three days ago and hasn't been heard from since." The note is signed, "Jeff."

The teacher, Mr. Draco, yells at you. "Give me that note!"

If you try to pretend that there was no note, turn to page 35.

If you walk up to the front of the class and hand the teacher the note, turn to page 36.

You are relieved when school is over. Just as you are about to walk out the door, the teacher, Mr. Draco, says: "Please stay after class. I like to have conferences with new students."

You wait nervously until the children leave, and then you begin to talk to Mr. Draco.

Halfway through the conversation, a fetid, foul stench invades the room.

If you want to get out of there and away from the stench, no matter what the consequences, turn to page 57.

If you think it is better to finish your conference with Mr. Draco in spite of the smell, turn to page 37.

You see a woman rush out the door of a nearby building. You watch as she puts a gun into her purse. Then you see the birthmark on her face. It is Ima Sneke. She is running toward the parking lot.

Turn to page 38.

As you walk among the buildings on the lot, you notice a peculiar smell. At first you think it is rotten eggs. But then you suspect it is sulfur, an ingredient that might be used in making the pellets.

You track the odor to a building at the far end of the lot. You open a door and follow the nauseating smell down a long, dark corridor. Suddenly, you stop.

(continued on page 24)

In front of a steel door are two huge Doberman pinschers. Their teeth are bared, and they are growling at you.

If you try to approach the dogs, turn to page 39.

If you think it would be wiser to back off and devise an alternate plan, turn to page 40.

You walk outside and approach the first man you see.

"Excuse me, sir," you inquire politely. "There was some shooting here a little while ago. Did you hear it?"

"As a matter of fact," the man says with a smile, "I did." He reaches under his jacket and pulls out a gun. "Let me introduce myself. My name is Wiley Fox. And I know you, Triple-O-Three. Now, come with me."

You have no choice.

Turn to page 41.

"Will it hurt?" you ask.

"You shall not feel anything. Merely lie down on this table, if you please," says the alien. She points a smooth webbed hand toward a tabletop suspended in midair.

You climb onto the table. It is soft. Your head is placed gently in a warm metal holder. And then, from out of the ceiling, a globe appears and moves silently and slowly back and forth over your body.

"Now," asks one of the aliens in a gentle but mechanical voice, "may we extract some of the red fluid from your body?"

If you detest the thought of giving them your blood, turn to page 42.

If you allow them to continue their experiments, turn to page 43.

Within seconds, the ship has transported you to the edge of your galaxy. You look through the giant portholes and are awed by the beauty of the Earth disappearing before your eyes. The black sky is dotted with billions of glowing stars.

You watch in silence until finally you cannot contain your curiosity any longer.

(continued on page 29)

"Who are you? Where do you come from?" you ask.

"We are Moosers from the Beegon galaxy," one of the aliens explains. "Ours is a peaceful planet, and we are interested in research." He then asks you to tell him about Earth. You explain about rivers and rainbows and the fish in the seas. You are truly enjoying yourself, when you look out the porthole and see a bright disc moving on a collision course toward your ship.

Turn to page 45.

You push the button, and suddenly you are surrounded by small silver-skinned creatures with bald heads. The most extraordinary thing about the creatures is the color of their eyes: an iridescent purple.

"Thank you," says the voice of one of the creatures.

You realize, to your amazement, that his mouth did not move when he spoke. Yet, the words appeared very clearly inside your own head.

"We are Gorks," says the voice of another. "We communicate by thought transmission. There is no longer any need for spoken language."

(continued on page 31)

Your head throbs and your eyes ache. You do not know what is happening.

"We have chosen you to help us accomplish our mission on Earth," says a Gork voice inside your head.

You watch as a sliding door opens.

"With the Gork power we are going to give you, you will be in control of everything that you see here. And that is just the beginning. Soon, the planet Earth will bow at your feet."

If the idea of all that control excites you, and you wish to accept the Gork power, turn to page 46.

If you fear the consequences of accepting such powers and try to escape through the open door, turn to page 50.

You dash up the stairs, but the voice is still with you. "There is no escape," it says.

Opening a door that you hope is some sort of exit, you are surprised to find a room full of motionless people.

"Escape now if you can," says one of the people. "We are helpless. The Gorks have taken away our ability to move. All we can do is speak."

"Who are the Gorks?" you ask.

"Aliens who want to take over the planet. They are evil."

Just then you hear movement on the stairs.

If you hide behind the control panel in the middle of the room, turn to page 51.

If you remain in plain sight and pretend that you are one of the statue-people, turn to page 52.

"We are Gorks," says a voice in your head. "You will do as we say."

You know that the aliens are communicating with you. But they have only slits for mouths, and you do not see the slits move.

"Stand up," orders the voice in your head.

If you decide you have no choice and should do as they say, turn to page 53.

If you think you might be able to fool them by pretending that you are unconscious, turn to page 54.

You stand up and offer your hand in greeting to the closest creature.

"Do not move," says the voice in your head. Although you do not understand how, you know that these creatures are communicating with you through thought transmission.

"Do not move," the voice repeats. "We are here to conquer Earth, and you are going to help us."

Turn to page 55.

"What note?" you ask. "There's no note."

"I hate liars," Mr. Draco screams. "You and Jeff will both remain after school."

You are frightened by the maniacal gleam in Mr. Draco's eyes as he speaks to you.

If you stay after school to meet Mr. Draco, turn to page 56.

If you rush out of the classroom as soon as the bell rings, turn to page 57.

You walk slowly to the front of the class and hand the teacher Jeff's note. After Mr. Draco reads the note, he crumples the paper and stuffs it into the wastebasket.

Then, with a grim smile, he tells the class that he has just spoken to Lisa's mother and that she told him Lisa was sick with the flu.

"So now," Mr. Draco says, "you can sit down and stop your gossip."

As soon as you are seated, Mr. Draco turns to face the blackboard. Jeff hands you another note.

"Mr. Draco is lying," it reads. "I live next door to Lisa, and she really has disappeared. Let's follow him after school."

If you want to follow Mr. Draco with Jeff, turn to page 58.

If you don't want to go with Jeff, turn to page 59.

By the time the conference is over, you feel nauseated.

"Is anything the matter?" Mr. Draco asks.

"It's the smell in here," you answer weakly. "It's making me sick and dizzy."

"What smell?" asks Mr. Draco without a hint that he might be teasing. You notice that when he speaks, the awful smell becomes stronger.

You begin to feel even dizzier and realize that something terrible is happening to your body. . . .

Turn to page 60.

As Ima climbs into a yellow car, you jump on the motorcycle parked next to the phone booth and strap on your helmet. You notice that there are special attachments mounted on a panel between the handlebars. You hope they will be useful if you find yourself in trouble.

Soon, you are chasing Ima on the freeway, weaving dangerously in and out of traffic. When the first bullet passes by your head, you realize that there is a passenger in Ima's car who is shooting at you.

You look down at the special control panel, wishing you knew what all the buttons meant.

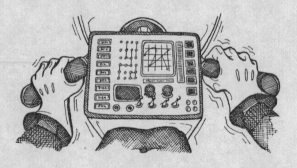

If you push the red button, turn to page 61.

If you think you should leave the buttons alone since you do not know what they will do, turn to page 62.

You reach into your shirt pocket and pull out a ball-point pen. Pointing it carefully at one of the dogs, you press the button on the end of the pen. You feel a jerk and then hear a hissing noise. The first dog falls to the ground as the tranquilizing dart hits. Then, pointing the pen at the second dog, you press again.

In seconds, the vicious dogs are fast asleep.

If you approach the door to see if it is unlocked, turn to page 64.

If you want to attempt to climb up the wall and look in the air vent to one side of the door, turn to page 65.

Remembering that you are wearing an electronic ring, you slip it off your finger and place it against the wall. Then, putting your ear to the electronic eavesdropping device, you hear two voices in the room on the other side of the wall.

"This is it," the woman's voice says. "The receptor pellets are completed. Let's go drop them in the reservoir."

"Aren't you going to take the antidote, Ima?" the man's voice asks.

"What do we need that for?" she asks with a wicked laugh. "In twenty-four hours every family in Los Angeles will be drinking our drugged water. And they won't even know it. Come on. Let's go."

You duck into the shadows as they come out of the room, and you watch as the man and woman lock the dogs in a cage and then walk away.

If you want to break into the lab and search for the antidote, turn to page 66.

If you choose to follow Ima Sneke and her companion, turn to page 67.

As you walk, you feel the barrel of the gun poking into your ribs. Wiley directs you through the door of a dingy building, down a long corridor and finally into a foul-smelling laboratory.

"I found him," Wiley says triumphantly to a woman.

You see the heart-shaped birthmark on her cheek and know that she is Ima Sneke. There is another man in the room. He is huge and has a stainless steel arm. You know that he must be Frank N. Stein. You are in a nest of vipers.

"Give us your weapons," the woman orders.

If you give them your weapons, turn to page 69.

If you try to stall, turn to page 70.

"I don't want to give you my blood," you say.

"It is not our wish to frighten you," the alien replies. "Instead, we shall leave you with our mark."

"What do you mean?" you ask. You feel a hot sensation on the back of your right hand. A red triangle appears.

You notice that all the aliens have triangles on their hands.

"That is the mark of our people. When we are nearby, you will see the mark clearly; when we are gone, it will fade. But, for the remainder of your days, the mark of the Moosers will keep you free from illness.

"And now," he says sadly, "you must go. Through astral projection we will relocate you to another time and another place. Farewell, my friend. Good luck."

Turn to page 7.

The medical Mooser is gentle. She places a metallic triangle on your wrist, and you watch in amazement as a tiny bottle next to the table fills with your blood. There are no needles. It is painless.

"You have been most cooperative, for which we must thank you," she says. "But now, you must make a choice. It is the most difficult choice of all."

(continued on page 44)

"We would like to take you back with us to our planet," she says to you in a gentle voice. "We cannot tell you when, but we promise to return you to Earth someday."

You long to experience life on another planet. But you are afraid that if you go, you might never see your home again.

You may go home now and tell your friends about your extraordinary experience. You hope that they will believe you.

The End

However, if you want to embark on the awesome journey to the Moosers' planet, turn to page 71.

An alarm siren wails, and the Moosers rush frantically to their stations.

"That is our enemy," explains the leader. "We did not intend to involve you in this. It is our battle, not yours. You must make a decision immediately. Both choices are dangerous.

"Through astral projection, we can try to place you back on the movie lot where the suspense movie is being filmed. Or you can stay with us while we wage combat with our enemy."

If you choose to return to the movie lot, turn to page 6.

If you would rather stay on the ship, turn to page 72.

You nod, indicating that you will accept the power. Then, to your astonishment, small antennae rise from the centers of their bald heads. Your body feels tingly; your eyes start to burn. Then the burning stops.

You look at your reflection in the smooth metallic walls of the spaceship and discover that your eyes have turned iridescent purple.

(continued on page 48)

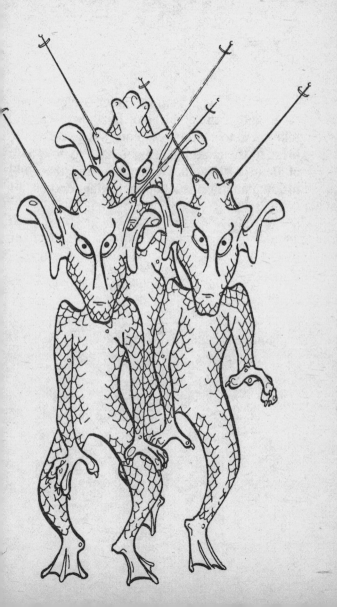

"Our mission," says the voice in your head, "is to gather the children of Earth together and take them to our planet. Your assignment is to bring us the children. All you have to do is look at them with your Gork eyes, and they will follow you. You shall be their king forever."

(continued on page 49)

"But what about the adults?" you ask.

"When you look at *them*," he answers, "they will fall unconscious."

If you like the idea of being king, turn to page 73.

If you think the children might be homesick on the planet Gork, and you do not want to take them away, turn to page 74.

You jump through the door and fall fourteen feet to the ground. As you land, you hear a cracking sound, and an agonizing pain shoots through your leg. It is broken, and you cannot run away.

Turn to page 75.

You are shocked to see from your hiding place that the first person to enter the room is your tour guide. He is dazed and frightened. He is followed by a strange, silvery creature.

Walking straight to the control panel, the creature carefully turns the biggest dial all the way to the right. Without a word, the tour guide takes his place among the statue-people. Then the alien leaves.

If you suspect that turning the dial in the opposite direction will free the people, turn to page 76.

If you think your chances are better if you try to escape and bring help, turn to page 77.

You stand perfectly still, pretending to be one of the statue-people. A small silvery being enters the room with a young girl. He walks to a console in the middle of the room and turns a dial. Then he leaves.

The girl cannot move. You attempt to help her, and it is only then that you realize that you, too, have been turned into a living statue.

The End

Shaking with fear, you stand up.

"What are those objects you are pointing at me?" you ask.

Before you have even finished the question, you know the answer. They are holding quasaps, multifrequency laser guns that can be used to stun or kill a victim.

Without even trying to resist, you throw up your hands. "I give up," you say hopelessly.

"We had heard that earthlings would be docile victims. But we did not know it would be this simple," says the voice. "We need slaves, and you are our first."

The End

You lie on the floor, knowing that you cannot defeat these creatures by force. As you lie there, you try to think of a clever way to save yourself.

If you try to block out the voice in your head, turn to page 78.

If you want to try to confuse the aliens, turn to page 79.

You know that you must not allow such a hideous act to take place. You pretend that you do not hear their instructions. Avoiding any sudden movements that might provoke the Gorks, you walk slowly toward the controls you have spotted on the other side of the room.

Just as the creatures lunge at you, you reach out and pull the first lever that you can touch.

There is a sudden jerk, and you feel the ship lifting off from the ground.

The voice in your head speaks angrily. "Because you pulled that lever, we are forced to depart from your planet. It will be years before we can return."

You are proud that you had the courage to save the planet Earth and its people. And you hope that someday you will find a way to save yourself.

The End

After school, you and Jeff talk to Mr. Draco. He says that you each must write, "I will not lie," five hundred times on the blackboard.

By the time you finish this task, it is dark outside.

"You have done a good job," Mr. Draco says. His pale, pasty face makes you uncomfortable; and you do not like the red glint in his eyes. "I would like to reward you for doing so well. Would you care to come have pizza with me?" he asks.

"Sure," Jeff answers immediately. "I'm starved."

If you join Mr. Draco and Jeff for pizza, turn to page 80.

If you think Mr. Draco is weird and decide to decline the invitation, turn to page 81.

You dash out of the classroom, not knowing where you are going. You only understand that anything is better than being trapped with a crazy teacher.

You run across the movie lot, finally entering a set that looks as if it is from a space story.

Turn to page 18.

The sun has set by the time Mr. Draco comes out of the school building, and you are glad that Jeff is with you as you walk down the dark, lonely streets.

"He is going into the cemetery!" Jeff whispers, pointing to Mr. Draco.

If the thought of entering a cemetery at night frightens you, turn to page 82.

If you decide to hide behind a tombstone and see what happens next, turn to page 83.

Having decided that you want nothing more to do with Mr. Draco, you wave good-bye to Jeff.

It is dark when you leave school, and the only light you see is a curious blue light in the distance.

Following it, you wonder what it could be. When you walk closer, you see, to your amazement, that the light comes from a spaceship.

Next to the ship is an orange triangle. Curious about what it is, you decide to step over and investigate.

Turn to page 10.

When you wake up, it is dark. You do not know where you are, but there are strange shapes around you that look like tombstones.

"My name is Lisa," says a sweet voice. "Are you all right?"

"Are you the Lisa that used to be in Mr. Draco's class?" you ask.

"Yes," she answers. "But I don't have to go to school anymore. I can also stay up as late as I want. I can arrange the same deal for you."

If you think you would like Lisa to make these arrangements for you, turn to page 85.

If you feel that something strange is going on and don't want any part of it, turn to page 86.

You push the red button and feel a surge of energy as jet action propels your motorcycle past Ima's car. Now you are an even better target, and you know you must try to lose her.

Turning off at the next exit, you enter a road that winds along a cliff. Ima follows. Bullets are whizzing around you.

You reach down and push another button. You feel something happening, but you do not know what. Then you hear the hideous screech of tires.

Looking back, you realize that the button activated a device that created an oil slick on the road.

You watch as the yellow car careens out of control and heads directly for the cliff. Just as it is about to fly over the edge, the car is stopped by a boulder.

When the evil scientists emerge from their battered car, you are there with your laser pen.

"You have ruined our plans!" Ima shrieks.

"Yes," you say with a smile. "That was my intention."

You have saved the city of Los Angeles.

The End

You do the only thing you can think of: you begin to zigzag the motorcycle in order to make yourself a more difficult target.

After many miles, Ima's car turns off toward the reservoir. You follow. Ima stops close to the water and jumps out of the car. She is holding a bag of pellets in her hand.

(continued on page 63)

The man with Ima begins to shoot at you again. You are pinned down by fire and know that it is only a matter of time until you are dead.

Turn to page 87.

Tiptoeing silently, you approach the door and try the knob. The door is locked.

If you decide there is no alternative except to explore the air vent, turn to page 65.

If you knock on the door, turn to page 88.

You balance yourself against the wall while you reverse the soles on your shoes. Then you remove the heels and hold them in your hands.

Pressing the suction cups to the wall, you test their strength. They hold firmly.

Then you begin to climb slowly up the wall, feeling like a human fly.

When you reach the top, you peer through the vent and see a woman standing next to a long counter covered with test tubes. That must be Ima Sneke, you think.

If you want to stay and observe the woman for a while, turn to page 89.

If you go outside and wait for the woman to leave so that you can enter the lab when it is empty, turn to page 90.

After you cut a hole around the lock with your laser, you open the door.

Inside, there are bottles and beakers everywhere. You know that you have only seconds to find the antidote that will neutralize the pellets that are to be dropped into the reservoir.

You are searching frantically, when suddenly you see a bottle sitting apart from the others. "Antidote," says the label in clear red letters. The bottle is filled with small blue capsules.

You take the bottle and run to the motorcycle, fearful that you are already too late.

Turn to page 91.

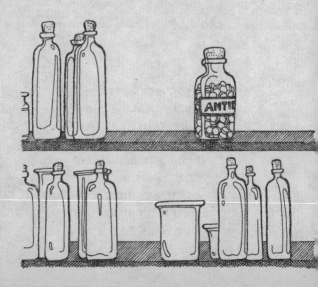

You follow Ima and her companion to their car. As soon as they climb in, you hop on the rear bumper of their car and lie across the trunk.

The car picks up speed as it moves through the lot. Once, as the car turns a corner, you nearly lose your balance. But you manage to hold on. Then the car hits a bump.

Helplessly, you roll off onto the side of the road.

The car roars into the distance as you lie there. Then there is silence.

A few minutes later, you hear strange, metallic voices. Looking around, you discover that you are surrounded by the three aliens whom you met when you first arrived at the studio lot.

They motion for you to come with them.

Turn to page 4.

One by one, you hand Frank your weapons: your wrist communicator, your laser pen, your suction-cup shoes, your sound-amplifying ring, your flame-throwing flashlight and your pencil-stiletto. You save the bubble-gum gas bomb for last.

Fumbling with the bubble-gum bomb, you deliberately drop it onto the floor.

"Pick it up," Frank orders, playing directly into your hands.

Instead of picking it up, you stomp down hard on the bubble gum. At the same time, you bite into the anti-gas pill that is hidden in your hollow tooth.

A strange smell permeates the room. Your companions will have a nice long sleep. And you know that when Ima and her cohorts wake up, the men from headquarters will take good care of them.

The End

You fumble with your wrist communicator, pushing the silent emergency alarm that will alert headquarters.

"Hurry up," says Frank, raising his steel fist in a threatening motion over your head. You know you must do as he says.

"Your arrival is timely," the woman says. "We were just discussing our need for a human guinea pig."

You shudder as she holds up two bottles.

"Choose one," she orders with a wicked gleam in her eye. "Drink it all."

If you drink the red liquid, turn to page 93.

If you drink the purple liquid, turn to page 94.

As you move away from Earth, you are overwhelmed by a kind of sadness. The beauty of your planet, growing silvery and small in the late afternoon sun, touches that part of you that longs to be home.

And yet, your regret is overshadowed by the adventures that lie before you, and the sure knowledge that someday you will return.

The End

Noises such as you have never heard careen off the walls around you, echoing painfully in your head long after they have ceased. Blinding lights flash, hurting your eyes with their white-hot intensity.

At last, there is one explosion more powerful than all the rest. The enemy has scored a direct hit on your ship. You are doomed.

The End

You walk down the steps of the spaceship toward a parking lot where you see a busload of children who have just arrived for a class trip.

One at a time, you look at them as they step out of the bus. You do nothing more. When the last child has left the bus, you turn and walk back toward the spaceship. Twenty-five children follow you as if you were the Pied Piper.

A teacher runs up to you. He is frantic with fear. "What are you doing?" he asks. "Stop!"

If you knock out the teacher with your Gork eyes and take the children to the ship, turn to page 95.

If the teacher's plea makes you question what you are doing, turn to page 97.

"I don't think I can do that," you say. "It would be cruel to take the children away from their families."

"We are sorry to hear that," says a voice in your head. "We had hoped you would cooperate. Now we shall have to find another earthling to do the job."

"I beg of you. Please," you say, "leave our planet alone. Let our children grow up and—"

"That is enough," interrupts the smallest Gork as he steps forward. "You are banished to the world of earthlings again, for you have abused the privilege of Gork power. Now we must take that power away from you. But you will live the rest of your life with purple eyes as a reminder of our encounter."

The End

Suddenly, the air is filled with sharp bursts of wailing noises followed by blinding flashes of light.

Looking up, you see that the Gork spaceship is surrounded by Moosers.

There is an earth-shaking blast and the spaceship disintegrates.

One of the Moosers approaches you.

"Thank you for saving my life," you manage to utter.

"Thank you for distracting the Gorks so that we could surround their ship," the Mooser replies.

You begin to cry from the severe pain in your leg. Then the Mooser reaches down and touches you gently on your knee, and the pain miraculously disappears. And so do the Moosers.

The End

You look at the control panel and reach down slowly. "No! Don't touch it!" someone yells. "Yes! Go ahead! It's the only chance we've got," another person says.

You place your fingers on the dial and turn it all the way to the left.

For a moment the room is quiet. Then a surprised voice says: "You've done it! We can move!"

"I know a way out," another says. "Follow me."

Someone else says: "And once we are out, I can destroy the ship with this quasap gun I stole. We are free! You have saved our lives!"

The End

You run quickly to the door and open it. You are face to face with the alien.

You turn to run, but it is too late. You feel a hot, piercing sensation in your back. You have been shot by a quasap gun. You will be dead in three seconds.

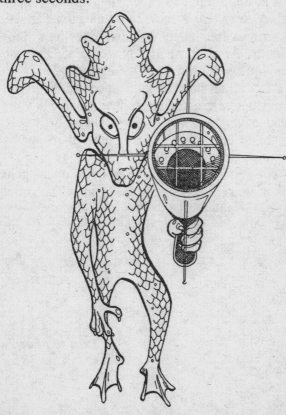

The End

"Now," says the voice, "let us cleanse this earthling's brain and reprogram it with our plan to enslave the Earth."

Frantically, you fill your head with your own thoughts. "A-B-C-D-E-F-G," you say to yourself in an attempt to block their transmission. "Two times two is four, two times three is six, two times four is eight; thirty days hath September, April, June and November; Oh, say, can you see by the dawn's early light . . ."

After a half hour of this concentrated effort, you stop, exhausted. You hear a voice in your head say: "We made a mistake. Throw the earthling out. This is not a mind that can be reprogrammed."

You close your eyes. When you open them again, you are relieved to find yourself near the set of the spy movie.

Turn to page 7.

You lie on the floor for a moment, trying to figure out how to baffle the Gorks.

An idea pops into your head. You jump up and stick out your tongue and cross your eyes and wiggle your ears. Then you do three back flips in a row and end by cartwheeling around the room.

The Gorks shake their heads in disbelief as you stomp around the room like an elephant, swinging your arms as a trunk. Just as you are about to hop like a kangaroo, the Gorks pick you up and fling you out the door.

The last words you hear are: "This earthling is too dumb for our purposes. It has the IQ of a toad."

The End

Sitting in the pizza parlor with Jeff and your teacher, you inquire, "Aren't you going to eat, Mr. Draco?"

"I never did like pizza," he answers. "I'll eat later."

He watches while you and Jeff eat a sausage and meatball pizza. You do not like the way Mr. Draco is staring at you. His face looks even more pale; and he is holding his lips in a weird way, as if he is covering up something in his mouth.

As soon as you finish, you excuse yourself. As you are going out the door, you hear Mr. Draco say, "It's dark out, Jeff. "I'll walk you home."

Turn to page 99.

You walk alone down the dark street.

"Psst!" You hear a voice call to you: "Hey, kid. I want to make you an offer you can't refuse."

"What is it?" you ask.

"There's ten thousand dollars in this envelope. If you deliver it for me, you can keep five thousand."

If you decide that this really is an offer you can't refuse, turn to page 101.

If you decide you would rather join Mr. Draco and Jeff for pizza after all and get away from this strange man, turn to page 80.

"There's no way I'm going to walk into that cemetery," you tell Jeff with conviction.

"Me, neither," Jeff says. "Would you like to come home with me?"

You may go home with Jeff and end the adventure here.

The End

Or, if you prefer, you can walk over to the set of the spy movie and get out of this place filled with missing people, strange teachers and cemeteries. Turn to page 7.

You watch as Mr. Draco puts a whistle to his lips. He gives three short blasts and one long one.

There is a rumbling noise everywhere, and suddenly the graves around you begin to open.

There is no way out. You dare not move.

Turn to page 102.

You are tired of everyone's telling you how late you can stay up. And you are sick of going to school every day.

"Sounds terrific," you say to Lisa. "Will you do it now?"

"Are you absolutely certain you want to go through with it?" Lisa asks.

"Yes," you answer with conviction, relieved that you will never have to look at a fraction or a decimal again.

Lisa smiles, revealing two long, sharp canine teeth. When you see her clawed hands reach toward your shoulders, you want to run. But it is too late.

"You will like being a vampire," she says. "Hold still. It only takes one quick bite."

The End

"I'm sorry you're not interested in my offer," Lisa says. She turns away from you and calls, "Okay, guys. He's all yours."

Out of the shadows, you see strange shapes moving toward you. You hear hideous laughter as they close in. You can now see the clawed hands and the long, sharp teeth, and you realize that you are surrounded by a pack of vampires.

You close your eyes in terror, knowing you are doomed. Then, suddenly, there is a tremendous explosion. The sky flashes blue and then red and then orange. Finally there is silence.

"Cut!" yells a voice. "Okay, everybody. That's it for the day. We'll see you tomorrow at seven."

You watch in amazement as the vampires remove their costumes, pulling off their claws and taking the false fangs out of their mouths. And you realize that whatever caused the Reality Warp when you first entered the movie lot has been fixed.

You smile with relief, but you are happy to have been part of a Reality Warp. You cannot wait to tell your friends.

The End

There is no way out, you think. You are doomed.

Then you hear a low rumble and feel a jolt. Soon, the earth is shaking back and forth, and you realize that this is an earthquake.

You watch in horror as a huge crack opens up in the earth. Ima and her companion lose their balance and fall into the crack. Then the shaking stops.

"Help us!" you hear Ima call. "We can't get out!"

Knowing they will remain there until you bring help, you hop on your motorcycle and rush toward the police station. You are pleased to see that there is little damage in the populated areas of the city. And you smile as you think of how an earthquake saved Los Angeles.

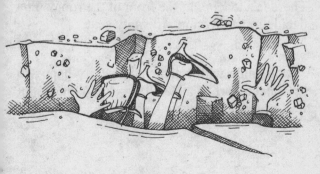

The End

You knock, not knowing what to expect. After a moment, the door is opened by a huge man. Looking at his arm, you see that it is made of heavy steel.

Glancing past the man, you see a woman standing next to a bubbling beaker of liquid. She has a heart-shaped birthmark on her face.

"Yeah?" asks the man.

"I'm looking for the cafeteria," you say.

"This ain't it," the man says.

Ima looks at you. "That's Triple-O-Three!" she screams.

You run, hoping that the great size of the man will make him slower than you. Not stopping to look back, you run until you have left the set of the spy movie.

Entering the first door you see, you find yourself in a schoolroom filled with students. There is a teacher at the front of the room. You decide to sit down in an empty seat.

Turn to page 12.

You watch as Ima speaks to someone out of your view.

"This is the final step," she says, adding a thick, gooey liquid to a beaker filled with a bubbling, yellow chemical compound. "Tomorrow the pellets will be ready, and we will take the first step toward conquering the world."

As the two liquids mix, a vile-smelling gas escapes and is sucked into the air vent.

Your eyes water, and you begin to choke and cough.

"Frank!" yells Ima. "Check out that noise."

The door bursts open before you can climb down. You feel a cold steel hand grab your ankle.

"Well, well, well," says the man with a sneer. "It looks like we won't have to worry about Triple-O-Three anymore."

The End

You stand in the shadows, waiting for Ima Sneke to come out of the building. After an hour, she emerges and walks briskly toward the parking lot.

If you want to break into the lab, turn to page 104.

If you would rather follow Ima, turn to page 38.

You jump onto the motorcycle and are at the reservoir in ten minutes.

(continued on page 92)

Just as you pull up, you watch in horror as Ima and the man dump the pellets into the water.

If you are confident of your aim and speed, and you think you can disintegrate the pellets with your laser before they hit the water, turn to page 105.

If you rush immediately to the water's edge and dump the antidote into the reservoir, turn to page 106.

If you first take out the stun gun from between the handlebars of the motorcycle and try to immobilize Ima and the man, turn to page 107.

You raise the bottle of red liquid to your lips and then hesitate.

"Try it, you'll like it," Wiley Fox says with a smirk.

Once again, Frank raises his fist.

You take a gulp and then swallow. You feel yourself growing faint. You know you are doomed. But you also know that the men from headquarters will arrive any minute. You have saved the world. Perhaps the men from headquarters can save you.

The End

Frank raises his fist in a threat, and you know that you must drink the purple liquid.

You swallow and feel slightly dizzy for a moment. Then you regain your senses.

"It doesn't work," Wiley says. "I told you so."

Just then, the door crashes down, and seven men from headquarters stomp into the room, their lasers trained on the culprits. They have responded to the silent alarm.

"Congratulations, Triple-O-Three," says the leader. "You have accomplished your mission."

The End

"You have done a good job," says a Gork voice in your head when you arrive at the ship with the children. "We shall deliver these children before collecting more."

Just as the spaceship is about to lift off, a high-pitched noise fills the air, and the cabin fills with Moosers, the aliens that you met earlier.

Each Mooser is holding a stun gun. You try to move but find you cannot. Everyone except the Moosers is frozen in position.

(continued on page 96)

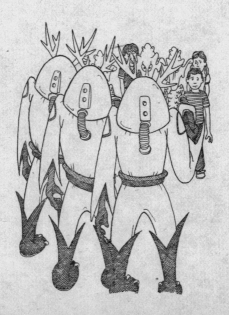

You watch as the Moosers pick up the children and carry them out. But they do not take you.

"We have come to save the innocent children," says the last Mooser when he finally speaks to you. "You lost your innocence when you chose to become a Gork. The consequences are dire: you shall be king of no one now. Instead you shall be a slave to the Gorks on their dark and forbidding planet."

The Mooser leaves, and you feel the spaceship lift off. There is no way out. You are now a slave of the Gorks.

The End

"What kind of madness is this?" the teacher cries out. "Why are you stealing our children? How can you do such a thing?"

You are about to look into his eyes when you realize that you do not want to harm him. You suddenly understand that you made a dreadful mistake when you accepted the Gork power. But you are afraid that you have come to your senses too late.

(continued on page 98)

Putting on your sunglasses to shield everyone from the power of your eyes, you tell the teacher that he and the children are in grave danger and that they all must leave immediately.

When they are gone, you run as quickly as you can away from the Gorks. You know that you will soon be safe. But you wonder sadly if you are destined to bear the eyes of the Gorks forever as a reminder of your very foolish choice.

The End

The next day at school, you wait for Jeff to arrive. But he never does. After class, you ask Mr. Draco, "Where is Jeff?"

"He must have been detained," Mr. Draco answers. "He left the pizza parlor right after you did, and I have not seen him since."

If you question Mr. Draco further, turn to page 108.

If you are suspicious of Mr. Draco and decide to follow him home, turn to page 109.

"That *is* an offer I cannot refuse," you say as you step into the shadows to take the envelope.

The stranger grabs you with two clawed hands. "You should have known better than to do that," the stranger says with a smile. And when he opens his mouth, you see two long, sharp canine teeth protruding from between his lips. You know without a doubt that the stranger is a vampire. You are doomed.

The End

In no time, Mr. Draco is surrounded by a group of people, both children and adults. They have risen from their graves.

"The topic for discussion this evening," says Mr. Draco, "is: Vampire Survival. Are there any questions?"

"What are the things that can kill us, Mr. Draco?" asks a girl in the front row.

"That's Lisa!" whispers Jeff.

"Shh! Let's listen!" you reply.

"As you all know, a wooden stake driven through the heart is our most common downfall. Fire, also, is dangerous," Mr. Draco answers.

(continued on page 103)

"And, although it is rare, we can also be killed if someone chops off our head with the blade of a spade from a gravedigger's shovel. Other than that, almost nothing can kill us; neither bullets nor knives nor blows to our heads. Of course, if we are sleeping inside our coffin, and someone nails the lid shut we obviously cannot escape."

"What about a cross?" asks one of the vampires.

"If the victim is holding a cross," Mr. Draco answers, "we cannot attack him. Now," he concludes, "if there are no more questions, let's go find dinner. Just remember to return before sunrise."

If you want to try to escape to Jeff's house, turn to page 111.

If you try to make it to the police, turn to page 112.

You reenter the building and walk quickly to the lab. With a tiny laser, you cut the lock.

You enter and move toward the brewing chemicals.

Just as you are reaching for the first beaker of liquid, a man's voice says, "Halt!"

Turning in time to see a steel fist heading directly for your chin, you send the man to the ground with one swift karate chop.

Pressing down the communicator button on your watch, you call headquarters. You know that within three minutes a team of specialists will arrive to dismantle the lab and take care of Frank N. Stein. Frank will lead them to Ima Sneke and Wiley Fox.

Your mission is completed.

The End

Pointing the laser pen at the pellets, you push the trigger.

There is a soft whoosh! as the pellets disintegrate. Then you point the laser toward the shocked man and woman.

"Don't move!" you order them.

They stand perfectly still.

Speaking into your wrist communicator, you contact headquarters and tell them to come immediately.

You know that this wicked pair will soon be behind bars where they belong. And you know, too, that you have performed a heroic deed.

The End

Without hesitating, you rush to the water's edge and dump the antidote into the reservoir.

Just as you finish, you hear the woman shriek: "You have destroyed my master plan! It will take years to repair the damage you have done!"

Then the man speaks to you: "You may have saved the city, but you forgot to save yourself. Now you will pay."

The End

As you are detaching the stun gun from its holster as quickly as you can, the man yells, "Freeze! or I'll shoot!"

You know that you are doomed. But you also know that you must save the people of the city.

Secretly gripping the antidote capsules in your hand, you toss them with all your might into the water.

Right after you hear the splash, you hear the gunshot.

The End

"But, Mr. Draco," you say, "I heard you tell Jeff in the pizza parlor that you were going to walk him home."

"Are you questioning my word?" Mr. Draco asks in an angry voice.

"My parents have taught me always to seek the truth, even if I have to oppose authority," you answer in a very polite manner.

"You are being impudent," Mr. Draco replies. "Get out of my class!"

If you decide that the only way to discover the truth is to follow Mr. Draco after school, turn to page 109.

If you try to find out what happened to Jeff, turn to page 113.

You wait outside the school until Mr. Draco comes out. It is dark, and he does not see you following him.

His house is set on the edge of town, and you do not like walking into such a dark, lonely spot.

After Mr. Draco goes inside, you run around the house and look into a lighted window.

You watch Mr. Draco enter the room and walk toward an object in the corner. He opens his mouth in an evil grin as he reaches out to touch it.

Horrified, you cannot believe your eyes. It is such a terrible sight that you want to scream in terror.

Turn to page 114.

You wait until the group of vampires has dispersed, and then you and Jeff stand up and begin to run.

"My house is this way," Jeff directs you as you run.

Just as you reach the edge of the cemetery, you turn a corner and run directly into three vampires.

Turn to page 115.

You wait until the vampires have left the cemetery, and then you and Jeff hurry toward the police station.

Once you are out of the cemetery and into town, you feel confident enough to walk in the open.

"We'll be heroes," Jeff says securely.

"Nobody can get us now," you add. "We're safe!" And then, just to prove your point, you yell: "Hey, Vampires! Come and get us now!"

"You called?" asks a dark, ominous voice from the shadows. "I'd be happy to oblige you."

The End

You do not know Jeff's last name, so you begin your search by going to the police.

At the station, the officer in charge informs you that Jeff has been murdered.

Your hands are shaking when you tell the police about Jeff and Mr. Draco.

They thank you for the information and send you home where you will be safe.

Two weeks later, the police officer calls to tell you that they have found conclusive evidence that Mr. Draco was the murderer. They congratulate you on your good judgment in reporting what you knew. "No one knows how many lives you have saved," he says.

The End

You stand perfectly still, too frightened to move. As Mr. Draco grins again, you see that his two canine teeth have grown long and razor sharp. As he reaches down and touches an open coffin, you notice that his fingernails have changed into claws. You cannot believe what you are seeing. Mr. Draco is a vampire!

Suddenly, Mr. Draco looks toward the window. His crazed red eyes glare at you.

"You will not escape with this knowledge!" Mr. Draco yells. And he runs out the door in order to catch you.

If you decide to run away as fast as you can, turn to page 118.

If you decide to hide in the bushes nearby, turn to page 119.

You look at the vampires. They are pale and gaunt, obviously hungry for their bloody nourishment.

"Aha!" says one, his lips spread in a grin over his long teeth. "I have always preferred children for dinner. Nothing like young blood, my mommy used to tell me."

(continued on page 117)

Desperate, you look around for help. Then you see a branch lying on the ground next to your feet. Stooping quickly, you pick it up and break it off at the bottom. You take the smaller piece and form a cross with the larger piece.

"Hold on to this with me!" you yell to Jeff.

He grabs it just in time.

Suddenly, an eerie screech fills the night as the vampires cover their eyes. "They know our secrets!" the vampires yell. And then they run away into the darkness.

You know now that you will be safe until you reach help.

The End

You have run only a few steps when you feel a clawed hand on your shoulder.

You are terrified. "I promise. I give my word that I won't tell anyone about you," you say, your heart beating faster.

"I like you," says Mr. Draco. "So I will give you a choice. Do you want to die, or do you want me to turn you into a vampire?"

"I don't know," you stutter, unable to think clearly.

"In that case, I shall make the decision for you," Mr. Draco says with a smile.

He leans toward you; his razor-sharp teeth move closer and closer to your neck.

The End

You remember reading that vampires run as swiftly as the wind, so you do not try to outrun Mr. Draco. Instead, you dive into the bushes, and he runs right past you.

You wait for over an hour until you think the coast is clear. You hope he is not waiting for you out there in the dark.

Finally, you decide that it is time for you to try to escape.

(continued on page 120)

You run as swiftly as you can to the police station.

You are afraid that they will not believe your story; but after you tell it to the officer, the policeman nods.

"I think you have solved a crime," he tells you. "We have found several people recently with two holes in their necks. We thought that they were dying from the bite of some strange snake. You have cleared up the mystery. We will pick up Mr. Draco for questioning immediately."

The policeman shakes your hand. "You have performed a heroic deed. Now we can all sleep safely again."

The End